For Sam, Helen and William S.W.
For Aki, Jeannie, Neelam and Dave Onion M.M.

TALK PEACE
by Sam Williams and Mique Moriuchi

Text copyright © Sam Williams 2005
Illustration copyright © Mique Moriuchi 2005

British Library Cataloguing in Publication Data
A catalogue record of this book is available
from the British Library
ISBN 0 340 88378 2 (HB)

First hardback edition published 2005
10 9 8 7 6 5 4 3 2 1

Published by Hodder Children's Books
a division of Hodder Headline Limited
338 Euston Road London NW1 3BH

Printed in China

Talk Peace

Sam Williams and Mique Moriuchi

h

*Hodder
Children's
Books*

A division of Hodder Headline Limited

Talk
soft.

Talk
loud.

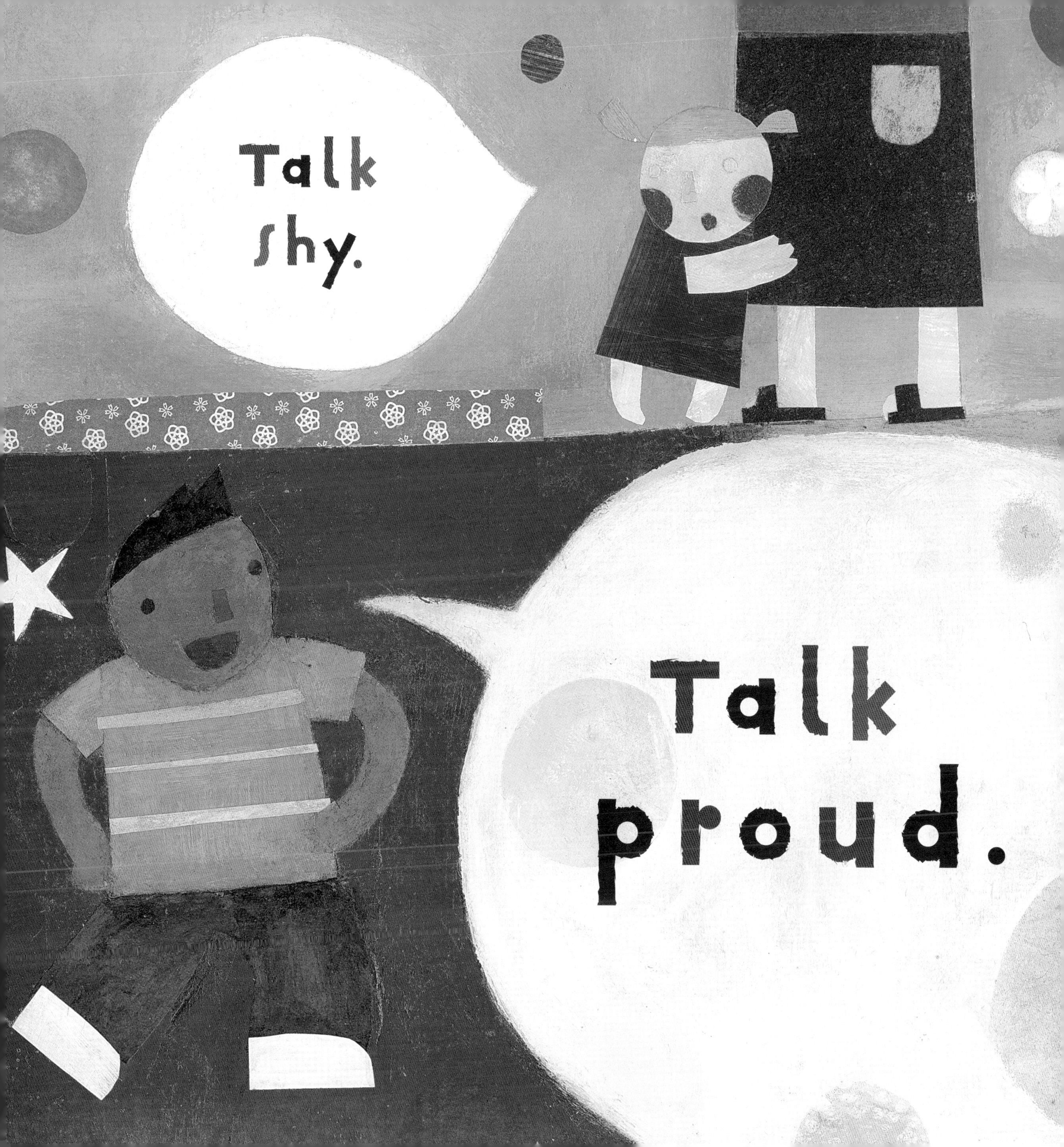
Talk shy.
Talk proud.

Talk
high.

Talk
low.

Way to go, talk peace.

on the breeze,
in the trees.

when you eat,

when you play.

In the day,

or at night,
in the light of a dream,

talk peace.

Look at race,

in the face,

any place,

anywhere,
don't scare,
talk peace.

When you party,
party jive.

Dance peace.

Talk peace.

On a train,
on a plane,

in the sun,   in the rain.

Understand

foreign land.

Take heart,
take part,

talk peace.

In a muddle,
when you huddle,

when you cuddle.

In a city, on the plain,

up the mountain, in the sea.

Two words on
the lips of the world,

talk peace.